Mossop's Last Chance

Michael Morpurgo
and
Shoo Rayner

Young Lions

For Anna

Two Hoots	Helen Cresswell
Desperate for a Dog	Rose Impey
Free with Every Pack	Robin Kingsland
Albertine, Goose Queen	Michael Morpurgo
Jigger's Day Off	Michael Morpurgo
Mossop's Last Chance	Michael Morpurgo
Hiccup Harry	Chris Powling
Ging Gang Goolie – It's An Alien!	Bob Wilson

First published in Great Britain
by A & C Black (Publishers) Ltd 1983
Published in Young Lions 1988
Eighth impression January 1992

Young Lions is an imprint of
the Children's Division, part of
HarperCollins Publishers Ltd,
77–85 Fulham Palace Road,
Hammersmith, London W6 8JB

Printed and bound in Great Britain by
HarperCollins Manufacturing, Glasgow

Chapter One

There was once a family of all sorts of animals that lived in the farmyard behind the tumble-down barn on Mudpuddle Farm.

At first light every morning Frederick, the flame-feathered cockerel, lifted his eyes to the sun and crowed and crowed, until the light came on at old Farmer Rafferty's bedroom window.

One... by one... the animals crept out... into the dawn... and stretched... and yawned. and scratched themselves; but no one ever spoke a word, not until after breakfast.

SSSHHH!

Mossop was a tired old farm cat who spent most of his day curled up asleep on the seat of Farmer Rafferty's tractor. Mossop paid no attention to Frederick – he got up when he pleased.

Farmer Rafferty was usually a kind man with smiling eyes, but like Mossop he was old and tired, and he ached in his bones in the wet weather. His animals were his only friends and his only family.

You look after me, and I'll look after you.

So, Frederick woke him up every morning.

Penelope and her speckled friends laid their eggs for him.

Auntie Grace and Primrose let
down their milk for him.

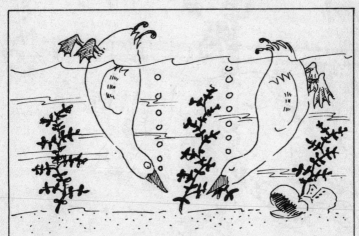

Upside and Down kept the pond
clear of weeds.

Captain carried him all around the
farm to check the sheep.

Jigger, the almost-always-sensible
sheepdog, rounded up the sheep.

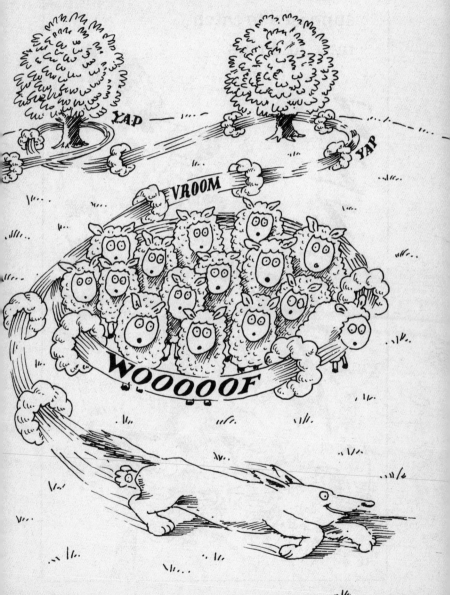

And Mossop was
supposed to catch
mice and rats.

Chapter Two

Farmer Rafferty always liked to sing as he worked. He sang in a crusty, croaky kind of voice.

iddley-pom-pom (whistle ♪♫) iddley-pom-tiddley-um-pom-la-la-la-di-di-doo-ho-ho-hum-I-tiddley-yum-tiddley-um-pom-tiddley-um-pom-yum

Hmmm! It's Beethoven's Violin Concerto today.

He's in a good mood today.

I like to hear him sing.

Now that's what I call music!

Dummy!

la-la-la- tiddley-um-pom pom-tiddley-um-pom-pom-

That morning though, as old
Farmer Rafferty went into the
tumble-down barn to fetch corn
from the corn bin, he suddenly
stopped singing.

with a hey and a ho and a tiddle-iddle-iddle-po-and-a-bing-bang-

Oh!

The animals crowded into the barn
to find out what was the matter.
They found Farmer Rafferty
standing by the corn bin holding a
mouse up by its tail.

This is a mouse, and there are
three more in there, Mossop.

Mossop!

Where is that Mossop?

Have we or have we not got a cat on this farm?' said Farmer Rafferty in the nasty, raspy voice he kept for special occasions.

'We have,' said Auntie Grace, the dreamy-eyed brown cow.

'She's right,' said her friend Primrose, who always agreed with her. 'We have, and he's asleep on the tractor seat.'

'Having a catnap,'
sniggered Upside
or Down – no one
could ever tell
which was which.

'Having his beauty sleep,'
mumbled Egbert,
the greedy, grumbly
goat who ate anything
and everything.
'Not that it'll help
him much.'

'Fetch him,' ordered old
Farmer Rafferty.
'Fetch that Mossop
here. I have a thing
or two to say to him.'

But at that very same moment Mossop wandered into the barn, yawning hugely.

Chapter Three

Mossop knew, and everyone knew,
that Farmer Rafferty always meant
what he said. So the whole day long
Mossop hunted

through the hay barns,

in amongst the barley sacks

and along the rafters.

But it was
no use, his
heart wasn't
in it.

He hadn't caught a mouse for a long
time now –

he was too old,

too blind,

too slow,
and he knew it.
Everyone knew it.

That evening, tired and miserable,
Mossop made his way back to his
sleeping seat on the tractor.

'How many did you catch, Mossop?'
asked Peggoty who lay surrounded
by her piglets on top of the steaming
dung heap.

Peggoty was a practical sort of a
pig. She could add up – which was
more than any of the others could.

'Catch anything, old son?' said
Jigger. Mossop shook his head.
'You've only got to say the word and
I'll give you a hand. Nothing would
give me greater pleasure.'

Captain's right, but thanks anyway Jigger. I'm too old.

Only got one eye and he doesn't work like he should.

And I'm slow as an old carthorse- begging your pardon, Captain. Anyway my claws are scarcely sharp enough to scratch myself.

As for my teeth- I've only got a few of them left and they're not much good anymore.

And all the animals – except one – gathered round the tractor because everyone loved Mossop.

But Albertine the goose sat on her
island in the middle of the pond,
and thought deep goosey thoughts.

Everyone agreed with Diana the
silly sheep, which made her very
happy.

'If Mossop can't see well enough,
then he should wear glasses,'
Auntie Grace said. 'That's what
Mr Rafferty does when he's reading.
He sees a lot better that way.'

But somehow that didn't seem to be
a good idea after all.

'If Mossop's claws aren't sharp enough, we could sharpen them up on Mr Rafferty's axe grinder,' said Peggotty. 'Mr Rafferty's axe always cuts better after it's been sharpened doesn't it?'

But Mossop didn't think that
sounded much fun either.

Jigger said.
'Mossop could have false teeth like
Farmer Rafferty. After all, old
Farmer Rafferty always eats a lot
better when he's got them in. He
keeps them on the kitchen window
sill. I've seen them.'

So they all went off to look at
Farmer Rafferty's teeth.

But in the end they decided it
wouldn't be fair on Mr Rafferty to
take his false teeth, and anyway
they were far too big for Mossop.

We must think harder. There's always a way round everything. We must think.

And so they thought.

Even Egbert the goat
tried to think, but he
found that a bit
difficult, so he ate a
paper sack instead.

Everyone thought . . . except Mossop,
who was far too tired to do
anything but sleep.

Chapter Four

Out on the island in the middle of her pond Albertine sat all by herself and thought deep, secret, goosey thoughts.

She rose to her feet, flapped her
great white wings and honked until
everyone gathered at the water's
edge in high excitement.

When Captain had calmed them
down, she spoke, and everyone
listened. They knew that Albertine
was a very clever goose.

Within minutes every mouse and every rat on the farm had gathered in the tumble-down barn.

Captain called the meeting to order, but the mice and rats all threatened to leave because Jigger was licking his lips.

Captain told Peggoty to sit on the dog's tail, just in case.

Albertine rose to speak.

Mice, rats and rodents all, welcome.

And she told them her master plan.
They listened hard – except for one
little mouse who was playing chase
in the corner with Pintsize,
the tiniest piglet.

'How many of you are there?' asked
Albertine politely, when she had
finished.

'A hundred and twenty-five, Guv'nor,
including the little'uns,'
said the spokesrat, after proper
consultations with the spokesmouse.

But Peggoty the practical pig knew
better.

A hundred and twenty-six
to be precise.

If you say so, Porker.

'Never mind. That will be quite
enough for what I have in mind,'
said Albertine, smiling.

Chapter Five

Mossop woke from his comfortable dreams on the tractor seat and saw the sun sinking through the trees. He knew the time had come for him to leave. Sadly he said goodbye to all his old friends.

Everyone was there to see him off except for Upside and Down who never missed their tea, not for anything.

There were tears in Mossop's eyes as he crawled under the farmyard gate for the last time.

MUDPUDDLE FARM

la-la-doobie-doobie-ho-ho-jingle-langa-dingle-dangle-la-la-la-la

'Of course he won't,' said Captain.
'He's happy again now. You can
hear him singing.'

Mossop made his way

across the vegetable patch,

in and out of the
runner bean sticks

and up to the back door.

He pushed the door open...

and padded down the hallway...

to the kitchen...

Where old Farmer Rafferty was sitting with his feet warming in the oven.

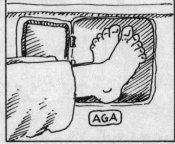

'Excuse me Mr. Rafferty, but
Captain says you wanted to see me
before I went,' said Mossop. 'I haven't
got any excuses Mr Rafferty.
I tried my best but I'm just not the
cat I was. It's age, Mr Rafferty,
old age. Well, I'll be on my way now.
Goodbye Mr Rafferty.

He took Mossop to the front
doorstep, and there in front of his eyes,
were row upon row of mice and rats.

They went right up to the goldfish
pond and round and back again.

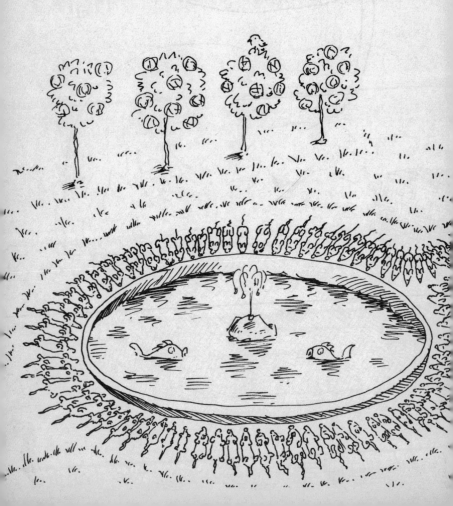

Mossop just stared and stared. He couldn't believe what he was seeing. Farmer Rafferty hung his old war medal around his neck.

> My Military Medal, this is. Present from one old soldier to another, and I've no one else I'd rather give it to. You're a brave old cat and I'm proud of you. Off you go now, back to the farmyard.

Farmer Rafferty went back inside the house shaking his head and muttering to himself.

Then one by one they stole off into the darkness until they were all gone.

And in return, we keep our old Mossop that everyone loves and who's so old and slow he could hardly catch a cold.
Only one thing to say, no other cat beside me ever had better friends, and that's a solemn fact.

And he smiled as only cats can,
yawned hugely, tucked his paws
neatly under his medal, closed his
eyes and slept.

The night came down, the moon
came up, and everyone slept on
Gigglewick Farm.